Samuel French Acting Edition

Bridal Terrorism

by Bill Rosenfield

SAMUELFRENCH.COM   SAMUELFRENCH.CO.UK

For Production Enquiries

United States and Canada
Info@SamuelFrench.com
1-866-598-8449

United Kingdom and Europe
Plays@SamuelFrench.co.uk
020-7255-4302

Each title is subject to availability from Samuel French, depending upon
country of performance. Please be aware that *BRIDAL TERRORISM* may
not be licensed by Samuel French in your territory. Professional and
amateur producers should contact the nearest Samuel French office or
licensing partner to verify availability.

MUSIC USE NOTE

Bridal Terrorism was first presented by Hofstra Unversity on October 20, 1988. It was directed by Miriam Tulin and Jeff Schaetzel. The cast (in order of appearance):

LIONEL STARK..........................Sean Lavin
MAY WILDER .... Juliette Stever
TERRY WINSHIP................... Kurt Engstrom
GINA   WILLIS.......................... Valerie Monti
BETTY   WILDER................ Carol Kastendieck
COLIN WILLIS .... Richard Omar

Scenic Design by Rob Weiner
Costumes by Ben Sander
Lighting by Maureen Root

This play is dedicated to Howard Siegman and to Miriam Tulin, with deep gratitude.

CHARACTERS

LIONEL STARK, an innocent man.
MAY WILDER, a bride.
BETTY WILDER, her mother.
GINA WILLIS, May's married younger sister.
COLIN WILLIS, her husband.
JUDGE TERRY WINSHIP, his boss.

TIME

A Sunday in May.

PLACE

A bench in Central Park.

*As the LIGHTS come up we see LIONEL, sitting
on the bench reading a book. He's an attractive
unassuming man in his late twenties/early
thirties.*
*MAY, an energetic, determined and not unattractive
woman, enters. SHE is wearing a beautiful
wedding dress and carrying three pieces of luggage.
SHE pauses for a moment, looking at Lionel—
sizing him up—and then approaches.*

MAY. Is it good?
LIONEL. (*Looking up from his book.*)
Hmmmm?
MAY. Is it good?
LIONEL (*Confused.*) I'm sorry?
MAY. The book? Is it good? Are you
involved?
LIONEL. No. Not really.
MAY. Then could I talk to you for a moment?
LIONEL. Well, to be honest, the book may not
be good but I'd like to get back to it. Get it over
with.
MAY. I'll make it worth your while.
LIONEL. Thanks, but no thanks.
MAY. Come on, be a sport.
LIONEL. Look, I don't wish to be rude but ...
I just want to read, ok? No offense?
MAY. No offense. I understand. I'll wait.

LIONEL. No. You don't understand. I don't want you to wait. I want you to leave. I want to read my book.

MAY. That you're not involved in.

LIONEL. Right.

MAY. I do understand, and I'll wait.

(*MAY begins to stare at him rather intently. LIONEL tries to read. But how can he with a woman in a wedding dress (with three pieces of luggage) staring at him? HE gives up.*)

LIONEL. All right. What is it?

MAY. I need your help.

LIONEL. I see.

MAY. Are you married?

LIONEL. No.

MAY. Are you involved in a serious relationship with a woman now?

LIONEL. No.

MAY. Are you involved in a serious relationship with a man now?

LIONEL. No.

MAY. How about communicable diseases?

LIONEL. How about them?

MAY. Do you have any? Have you been exposed to any?

LIONEL. Not that I know of.

MAY. Well, at this point you'll have to do.

LIONEL. Do what?

MAY. Help me out.

LIONEL. Do you want money? I don't have any money. I have a token. One token. I need it. Please. Isn't there someone else who can help you?

MAY. (*Begins to cry.*) No, not really.

LIONEL. (*Lowers his guard.*) Hey, I'm sorry I snapped. What's wrong?

(*The tears have vanished.*)

MAY. Could you stand up for just a moment?

LIONEL. (*Resisting.*) Well ... (*Relenting.*) Sure. Why not?

MAY. You'll do just fine.

LIONEL. You're not a mugger or something, are you?

MAY. Or something?

LIONEL. A terrorist of some sort?

MAY. Yes, as a matter of fact I am.

LIONEL. Oh.

MAY. I'm a bridal terrorist. (*SHE calls offstage.*) YO! Over here.

LIONEL. What are you doing?

MAY. Bridal terrorism. I'll explain in a minute. (*Calling offstage.*) Come on. Let's move it.

(*JUDGE TERRY WINSHIP enters. He is an older man, but very much in tune with the times.*)

TERRY. Found one?

MAY. Sure did.

LIONEL. One what?

TERRY. How do you do?

MAY. Judge Winship, this is ... I'm sorry, what's your name?

LIONEL. Lionel Stark. How do you do?

TERRY. Fine. You can call me Terry.

LIONEL. Right. What's going on?

TERRY. Shhh. May's in charge.

MAY. Where are the others?

TERRY. They were right behind me. I see your sister over there.

MAY. Leave it to her to be distracted.

LIONEL. Others?

TERRY. Members of the party.

LIONEL. Members of what party?

MAY. The wedding party, silly. (*SHE calls offstage again.*) GINA! COLIN! MOM! Jesus, you'd think they'd hurry.

TERRY. Would you like to start without them?

MAY. I've waited thirty-four years, I think I can wait four more minutes.

LIONEL. Excuse me. Is this a some sort of joke?

MAY. Far from it.

LIONEL. Is there a camera somewhere? Are you what's his name?

TERRY. Terry Winship. I'm the judge.

LIONEL. Right. But aren't you really that guy? You know, bald, kinda chubby? Really annoying? What *is* his name?

TERRY. Do I look bald, fat and annoying?

LIONEL. Well no. But ...

TERRY. I didn't think so. Do you have the rings?

LIONEL. Rings?

MAY. Colin has them.

LIONEL. Do I know any of you?

TERRY. I've told you, I'm Judge Terry Winship.

LIONEL. And who is this?

TERRY. That's your bride-to-be May Wilder.

LIONEL. My bride-to-be? Will someone just explain what exactly is going on?

(Before anyone can answer, GINA WILLIS, May's younger sister and a very pretty woman in her mid-twenties, enters.)

GINA. Mom broke a heel. Colin is helping her hobble. And I think you missed two live ones headed toward the reservoir. That is, if this one doesn't pan out. *(GINA looks Lionel over.)* So this is Mr. Right?

MAY. He might be, but for now he's just Mr....

LIONEL. Stark, Lionel Stark.

GINA. Pretty good, May.

MAY. I think so.

GINA. May Stark. Sounds nice. *(SHE fixes her hair.)* So introduce me already? *(To Lionel.)* Looking forward to being a victim?

MAY. Lionel, this is my sister, Gina Willis.

LIONEL. Hi. Not at all.

GINA. Not at all?

LIONEL. I'm not looking forward to it at all.

GINA. Too bad. Isn't this a beautiful day for a wedding?

LIONEL. Well ...

TERRY. I've never understood why June weddings are more popular than May ones, especially when there are days as sunny as this one.

MAY. Look, I'm going to go help Mom and Colin make sure he doesn't get away. At the rate they're going I *will* be an old maid. (*MAY runs off.*)

LIONEL. Listen, I don't mean to be rude but...

GINA. There is no proper etiquette for terrorists or their victims. Besides, how can you be rude? You're family. Almost.

LIONEL. That's what I wanted to ask about.

GINA. What is?

LIONEL. It looks to me like there is going to be a wedding very shortly.

GINA. The light dawns.

TERRY. A beautiful day for it.

LIONEL. Yes, it is. However, I ...

GINA. Please, Lionel. Wait a minute. I know what you're going to say but let me explain it to you.

TERRY. Gina, I think that's May's job.

GINA. (*Suddenly loud and hysterical.*) Oh my God, why is Colin walking like that? Terry, quick! Go help him!

TERRY. Yes. (*Runs off.*)

GINA. Ok, let me give it to you straight. There's about to be a wedding.

LIONEL. Who's getting married?

GINA. You are.

LIONEL. I am?

GINA. Yes. To my sister May.

LIONEL. I don't know her.

GINA. Yes you do. She's the one in the wedding dress walking toward us, holding a bouquet and yelling at our mother.

LIONEL. No. What I mean is that I don't *know* her, other than today.

GINA. How often do victims know their assailants? Right?

LIONEL. But ...

GINA. Shhh. Here they come now. Just go along with this. Everything will be fine.

LIONEL. But ...

GINA. Please. It'll work out. Everybody always has misgivings and doubts just before the ceremony. It's natural. I was a nervous wreck before I married Colin. Relax.

(*MAY and TERRY enter helping COLIN, a bookish man a few years older than GINA, and BETTY WILDER, a woman in her late fifties. COLIN is limping and BETTY is out of breath.*)

MAY. Mom, just sit on the bench and relax.

BETTY. How can I relax? This is the happiest day of my life.

COLIN. I hate wearing good shoes in the park. Something always gets underneath my foot.

GINA. I have a good idea what.

TERRY. Are we pretty close to beginning?

MAY. Just give me two minutes and we're all systems go.

LIONEL. May?

MAY. Not now, Lionel. There are a thousand details to take care of. Here, put this on. (*MAY hands Lionel a boutonniere.*)

COLIN. Do I have the rings or do you?

GINA. You do, dear. I'm the maid of honor; you're the best man.

COLIN. And is this the lucky guy?

GINA. Indeed he is. Lionel Stark, this is my husband, Colin Willis.

MAY. Gina! Cut the small talk. I need you.

GINA. Excuse me. I'll be back in a moment.

LIONEL. How do you do?

COLIN. Fine thanks. Pretty exciting, isn't it?

LIONEL. Exciting?

COLIN. Yeah.

LIONEL. Well, it's all so sudden.

COLIN. It's a shame we hadn't met before today. Otherwise, I would have thrown you one helluva bachelor party.

LIONEL. Really?

COLIN. Sure, we'd have gotten the old gang together. Talked about the good old days, maybe brought in a few hookers. It would have been great.

LIONEL. Maybe some other time?

COLIN. You bet.

TERRY. Excuse me, Lionel do you have anything that you'd like to be interpolated into the ceremony?

LIONEL. Like what?

COLIN. Last rights?

LIONEL. (*Horrified.*) Last rights?

COLIN. Just kidding.

TERRY. Something that perhaps you find comfort in? A poem? A song?

COLIN. A sedative.

LIONEL. Why'd you say that?

COLIN. Just kidding. I'm a kidder.

LIONEL. I think just the ceremony itself, I guess.

TERRY. Good. Sometimes people have a favorite song they want to sing and stories they want to tell. One time I married two clowns—they exchanged pies.

LIONEL. I see.

TERRY. May? Gina? Betty?

MAY. Ready.

BETTY. My oldest baby, a wife at last!

COLIN. Here we go.

LIONEL. Wait just a minute. Aren't we rushing things a bit here?

MAY. Shhh. Lionel. Be patient.

GINA. Colin, hurry and turn on the music, for Christ's sake.

COLIN. Oh, right. (*COLIN takes out a cassette player and presses the play button.*

MENDELSSOHN'S WEDDING MARCH comes on.)

TERRY. Lionel you stand here. Colin next to him.

LIONEL. Gina I ...

GINA. Lionel, trust me. Just go along with it. It's all for the best. Submit for the sake of all mankind, ok?

COLIN. (*To anyone.*) Here?

TERRY. Fine. Betty, you come first.

BETTY. Mothers always come first.

GINA. Spare us. Will ya, Ma?

TERRY. Followed by Gina and then finally, May.

(*THEY all walk from one side of the stage to where COLIN, TERRY, and LIONEL are standing. MAY looks lovingly at LIONEL who smiles back. COLIN stops the MUSIC.*)

TERRY. This will make a swell wedding picture.

MAY. Terry?

TERRY. Yes?

MAY. The ceremony.

TERRY. Right. Dearly beloved, we are gathered here today in the beautiful spring sunshine to bring together these two people, May Wilder and Lionel Stark, in matrimony. If there is anyone among us who has reason that these two should not be wed, let him speak now or forever hold his peace.

LIONEL. Uh-hem.

MAY. Lionel. Shhh.

TERRY. Do you wish to say something?

LIONEL. Err ... Yes. I do.

MAY. Don't say "I do" yet. Wait until he asks the question.

LIONEL. No. No. I don't do. I mean I don't know if I do, but I do have something to say.

BETTY. I knew this would happen.

LIONEL. Um ... I don't know you. Any of you. I was just sitting on the bench reading. And now it seems I'm getting married.

TERRY. Yes, go on.

BETTY. He's got a lot going on up there.

MAY. One of the essential ingredients in terrorism is the element of surprise.

LIONEL. Is this a joke?

MAY. (*Very seriously.*) Lionel, marriage isn't a joke. To anyone.

LIONEL. I know that but I think *this* marriage just might be different.

TERRY. Last minute doubts are common, Lionel.

LIONEL. These aren't last minute doubts. These are *first* minute doubts.

MAY. I see. So you're saying that you don't want to get married?

LIONEL. Right.

MAY. (*Thinks for a moment. Then:*) You're the victim. You don't have a choice.

COLIN. I knew this wouldn't work.

BETTY. (*To Lionel.*) Troublemaker.

GINA. Mom. Please? It will. Now shhhh.

LIONEL. Could all of you just go away for a minute and let me talk to May? Or whoever it is that's in charge?

BETTY. A bum. I knew he was a bum from the start.

MAY. Mom, please.

BETTY. What kind of husband is she going to meet in the park?

GINA. Where did you meet Daddy?

BETTY. In a bar.

GINA. Ma, do you ever listen to yourself?

BETTY. Yes.

MAY. Lionel's right. Would all of you just go away for a minute?

TERRY. Where are we supposed to go?

MAY. Why don't you all get a hot dog or something?

BETTY. And spoil our appetite for the reception?

MAY. Mom, please?

BETTY. Ok. Come on, let's go look at the birds.

COLIN. I hate birds.

GINA. We'll just be over there. If you need anything. Ok?

MAY. Thanks.

(*EVERYONE goes off. Leaving LIONEL and MAY alone.*)

LIONEL. Well I ...

MAY. Please. We don't have much time.

LIONEL. It's just ...

MAY. If you aren't going to help me then I have to know now.

LIONEL. I want to help you. I don't *know* you, but I want to help you.

MAY. Thanks.

LIONEL. I'm willing to help you. But marriage? Isn't that asking a lot?

MAY. Ok. Let's forget all of them for a minute and do it ourselves.

LIONEL. Do what ourselves?

MAY. Please just put this ring on.

LIONEL. What ring? You're not holding anything.

MAY. Pretend. Colin has the real one.

LIONEL. All right.

MAY. Now repeat after me: With this ring ...

LIONEL. With this ring ...

MAY. I Thee wed ...

LIONEL. I Thee wed ...

MAY. To have and to hold from this day forth...

LIONEL. Wait a minute.

MAY. Please, there isn't much time.

LIONEL. But I think ...

MAY. TO HAVE AND TO HOLD ...

LIONEL. To have and to hold...

MAY. From this day forth ...

LIONEL. From this day forth ...

MAY. Til death do us part ...
LIONEL. Til death do us part.
MAY. Now you give me this ring.
LIONEL. What ring?
MAY. Pretend. For Christ's sake.
LIONEL. Here.
MAY. With this ring I thee wed. To have and to hold from this day forth til death do us part.

(*MAY kisses Lionel.*)

MAY. Mrs. Lionel Stark. I like that.
LIONEL. I just want to know what this is all about.
MAY. I just couldn't stand it anymore. It was time to take some positive action.
LIONEL. Stand what?
MAY. Being single.
LIONEL. Oh.
MAY. I wouldn't mind being an old maid if I were older, but right now in these God-awful middle years it's like I don't know who I am or what I'm doing. But the BTP put a lot of things into focus for me.
LIONEL. The BTP?
MAY. Bridal Terrorism Party.
LIONEL. I don't understand.
MAY. There was this study a couple of years ago that said a woman over the age of thirty-five would more likely be the victim of a terrorist attack than get married. The BTP was formed to

make that report false. There is a eighty-seven percent success rate in the BTP marriages.

LIONEL. Really?

MAY. Really. In the orientation program we are trained to spot certain characteristics that are ideal in a husband.

LIONEL. And you spotted those in me?

MAY. Of course.

LIONEL. Like?

MAY. I'm not at liberty to say. But rest assured we don't just settle—we choose our victims carefully.

LIONEL. But maybe if instead of picking out someone you don't know, you might have met someone who you connected with?

MAY. It hasn't happened yet.

LIONEL. Ever?

MAY. Oh, a few close calls along the way, but I like this idea better.

LIONEL. But marriage?

MAY. It'll help me put my life into focus. Desperate times call for desperate action.

LIONEL. I see. And marrying me will help?

MAY. It just might.

LIONEL. I suppose I should give it time.

MAY. It's always important to give new things a chance.

LIONEL. Right.

MAY. So marriage will be new to both of us, right?

LIONEL. Right.

MAY. We'll be starting our life together. Where do we live?

LIONEL. We?

MAY. Yes, where do we live?

LIONEL. Well, I'll tell you quite frankly I'm not inclined to go along with this.

MAY. I see.

LIONEL. I think that I'm just going to walk away from here, ok?

MAY. I don't think that's a good idea.

LIONEL. Your sister said there were two possibilities over by the reservoir. Why don't you check them out?

MAY. My mind's made up.

LIONEL. Sorry I can't help you.

MAY. You can and you will. (*MAY produces a gun.*)

LIONEL. Oh.

MAY. So where do we live?

LIONEL. Well ...

MAY. Now you'll take me seriously, won't you?

LIONEL. You'll have to excuse me, I've enjoyed being part of your therapy but I think you should put that away and let me leave. I have better things to do today than to marry a bridal terrorist.

MAY. Come on! What are you doing sitting alone in the park on a beautiful Sunday in the spring reading? You know as well as I do that you should be with your wife, or mistress, or girlfriend. Right?

LIONEL. I like being alone and outside.

MAY. What'd you do last night?

LIONEL. I ... had dinner with some friends.

MAY. Did you have a date?

LIONEL. No, these were just friends. People like myself.

MAY. Lionel, aren't you tired of being single and straight in New York?

LIONEL. Well, of course, sometimes I get depressed.

MAY. You start thinking, is there no one in this world for me? Am I doomed to spend the rest of my life alone?

LIONEL. Sure. That happens.

MAY. Me too. But you see, I've solved that problem for both of us.

LIONEL How?

MAY. We're married.

LIONEL. Not really.

MAY. We will be in a few minutes. I'll confess to you. I looked around for quite a while before I decided to ask you to marry me.

LIONEL. Really?'

MAY. Sure. We were all sitting at the entrance to the park for the better part of an hour before I headed in this direction.

LIONEL. I'm flattered.

MAY. Now I think you're a handsome guy, and I know you think I'm kind of pretty, otherwise you wouldn't have gone along this far. Right?

LIONEL. Well, yes.

MAY. So we have physical attraction going for us.

LIONEL. Sure.

MAY. When the ceremony is over we'll go to your place and make ourselves a honeymoon? Come on, be a sport! Whaddaya say?

LIONEL. I say you're crazy.

MAY. Who isn't?

LIONEL. True.

MAY. Your parents alive?

LIONEL. Yes.

MAY. Have they been pressuring you to get married?

LIONEL. A little. But they're in Florida so it's only once a week.

MAY They'll be thrilled for you. They can die happy now.

LIONEL. But I don't know you.

MAY. If you knew me, we'd date for a while, then we'd have a talk about commitment and all that other stuff, then we'd end up breaking up. We'd be even older than we are now and still be alone. Not a pretty prospect.

LIONEL. Not at all.

MAY. But now that we'll be married we've got something to hold on to. Something substantial, an emotional and moral commitment founded on the sacrament of marriage as an institution. With the help of the BTP workshops, our marriage will be an inspiration to millions of individuals like ourselves. Sure we'll have problems. But dammit, we'll work through them all. We'll make it work. We'll be stronger for it. For us and the kids.

LIONEL. The kids?

MAY. Of course we're going to have kids.

LIONEL. How many?

MAY. Just two.

LIONEL. I like kids.

MAY. If you want more than two you'll have to go somewhere else for them. I don't want more than two.

LIONEL. All right.

MAY. Maybe only one. We'll see how things go.

LIONEL. We'll see.

MAY. So ... wanna go have a honeymoon? Or (*Pointing the gun.*) do you wanna meet your maker?

LIONEL. You know, you're not entirely wrong.

MAY. I knew you'd see the light.

LIONEL. More than once I've broken up with someone because we were simply afraid of making that final (*HE chokes on the word.*) commitment.

MAY. And what held you back?

LIONEL The fact that it might be the wrong decision, or maybe knowing too much about one another.

MAY. So you made no decision. Right?

LIONEL. Right.

MAY. Well guess what?

LIONEL. What?

MAY. I'm here to make that decision for you.

LIONEL. (*A realization.*) I'm getting married.

MAY. *We're* getting married.

LIONEL. Wow. Things happen so quickly nowadays. And for the most bizarre reasons.

MAY. Are we going to your place for a honeymoon, or are we going to go straight to the reception?

LIONEL. Reception?

MAY. What's a wedding without a reception?

LIONEL. You're right.

MAY Reception first. Then honeymoon. Ok?

LIONEL. Don't I get to invite people too?

MAY. Sure. We can go to your place, get changed and while I'm unpacking you can make some calls and they can come to our wedding reception.

LIONEL. Where is it?

MAY. The Plaza.

LIONEL. Really?

MAY. Really. If you're gonna do it you gotta do it right.

LIONEL. What if you hadn't found a husband today?

MAY. I had to find a husband today or else I would have been a failure not only to myself, but to the party. Today is my wedding day. I didn't know who I was going to marry, but I knew that I was going to be married by four o'clock today, come hell or high water.

LIONEL. And you are.

MAY. And I am. So can we proceed?

LIONEL. Mrs. Lionel Stark.
MAY. Lionel?
LIONEL. Yes?
MAY. You may now kiss the bride.

(*THEY kiss, and it's a good one.*)

LIONEL. Wow.
MAY. Wow is right. (*MAY calls to the others.*)
Ok. Everyone. Come on back. He's gonna do it.
BETTY. The man is a saint. My daughter is
marrying a saint. This is the happiest day of my
life. Bar none.
GINA. Mom, please.
BETTY. What? I shouldn't be proud that my
little princess has found a saint to marry her?
GINA. Of course you should be proud. I only
want you to be proud of all of us.
COLIN. So you're going to go through with it?
LIONEL. Why not? It's a nice day. I don't
have to be back at the home until six-thirty.

(*MAY turns to look at him.*)

COLIN. Great. Plenty of time to stuff yourself
at the reception, and then maybe get in a quick
one.
LIONEL. Ok. I'm ready when you are.
MAY. Just a minute. (*To Gina.*) What did I
just hear?
GINA. Thunder?
MAY. No. Colin, could I talk to you privately?

COLIN. Sure, May.

MAY. What did Lionel just say?

COLIN. "Ok, I'm ready when you are."

MAY. No, before that.

COLIN. I said, "Great. Plenty of time to stuff yourself at the reception and then maybe get in a quick one."

MAY. And what did he say before that?

TERRY. Hey, what are we doing? Is there a wedding or not?

LIONEL. You bet. I'm game.

GINA. Terry, please be patient.

COLIN. He said, "Why not? I don't have to be back at the home until six-thirty."

LIONEL. That's amazing! How do you remember exactly what I said?

TERRY. He's my best court reporter.

LIONEL. You sit there at those cute little machines and write down everything that's said?

COLIN. Sure.

LIONEL. That must be a lot of fun.

COLIN. It is.

MAY. Lionel, when you say you don't have to be back at home until six-thirty is it because you have a roast in the oven?

LIONEL. No.

COLIN. May? You misquoted him. It's back at the home by six-thirty.

MAY. (*To Colin.*) Please? (*To Lionel.*) Is it so you can feed your cat? Please God let him have a cat!

LIONEL. No.

MAY. Lionel: Your home or the home?

LIONEL. My home is The home.

MAY. My worst fears confirmed.

GINA. Jesus, May! Do you think?

BETTY. A cuckoo bird. Typical. Of all the men in New York City, you have to decide to marry a deranged inmate who lives in some godforsaken halfway house.

MAY. Mom, please.

BETTY. Excuse me.

MAY. Lionel, where do you have to be at six-thirty?

LIONEL. At my home.

MAY. And your home is ...

LIONEL. (*Simply.*) My home is very special to me. Yes.

MAY. Oh God! I've married a nut case?

LIONEL. An out-patient, please.

GINA. Listen, you're not married. We'll go find someone else. No big deal. Come on everyone, we'll go find the cute joggers I saw over at the reservoir. Let's move it out.

TERRY. Wait a minute. This is a snag, but not an unsurmountable one.

MAY. (*Crestfallen.*) I can pick 'em. Even without knowing I can pick 'em, I can pick 'em.

TERRY. May, Gina, everyone, I think we should just attempt to clarify exactly what the situation is.

MAY. Jesus, Terry, it's very clear. I want to get married. I find Mr. Right and discover he isn't—he's from a loony bin. So I'm calling off the wedding and I'll find someone else.

TERRY. Need I remind you that marriage is a sacred institution and not to be treated lightly.

MAY. I understand that.

LIONEL. May honey, I'm getting better all the time. We can work through this thing together.

COLIN. Do you have a criminal record?

LIONEL. No, but I have every album Billy Joel ever made. Ba Dum Bum.

GINA. May, you must have some sort of divining rod that leads you to these guys.

MAY. I don't. I swear I don't.

BETTY. You're lying. First there was that bee keeper.

COLIN. I liked him.

BETTY. Then the soda jerk.

GINA. We all gained weight during that one.

BETTY. Then that car salesman.

MAY. Mom!

BETTY. It was just a matter of time before you settled on one direct from the loony bin as opposed to the ones that simply belonged there.

GINA. It was inevitable. Tough break, kid.

MAY. This is my wedding day. Why can't it be happy?

LIONEL. I've always felt that weddings weren't so much for the bride and groom as for the family. A chance to celebrate what a family means to each other.

MAY. Very well said.

LIONEL. Thank you.

GINA. Listen, Lionel. You seem like a nice guy and if you hadn't said anything about having to be at the home you'd be my brother-in-law right now and maybe in a few months at a cocktail party at our house you'd come and see if you could give me a hand in the kitchen and one thing would lead to another and you'd give me a hand somewhere else and because I would feel like trash cheating on my husband with my brother-in-law, I'd slap you across the face for being a creep and then I'd tell May what you did and she'd file for divorce, take you for every penny you've got and leave you.

LIONEL. Gee, you think so?

GINA. Yeah I do.

LIONEL. My God!

COLIN. Gina?

GINA. What?

COLIN. You said, "I would feel like trash cheating on my husband with my brother-in-law..."

GINA. And I would, Colin.

COLIN. That seems to imply that you wouldn't feel like trash cheating on me with someone else.

GINA. Oh. Well, I didn't mean to imply that.

COLIN. But that's what you said.

GINA. I'm sorry. Listen, Colin, I'm trying to make a point here to Lionel, so I'll get back to you in just a minute.

LIONEL. What's your point, then?

GINA. My point is that this marriage is doomed from the start. So why not just call all of this off and we'll continue our search for a husband for May.

LIONEL. Doomed? I think we have a chance at something positive here.

MAY. How can I face the other members of the party with an out-patient as a groom?

BETTY. May? Are you satisfied? You've created a monster.

LIONEL. Because I believe in marriage I'm a monster?

MAY. Lionel.

LIONEL. Because I'm willing to take emotional, heartfelt chances, I'm deranged?

MAY. Lionel, honey.

LIONEL. Because for the first time in a long time I meet a woman who isn't interested in what my past is, but only what our future together may hold, that makes me a cuckoo bird?

COLIN. Good point.

LIONEL. Which?

COLIN. About not interested in the past, only the future. I like that.

LIONEL. Thank you.

COLIN. You're welcome. Go on.

LIONEL. When I came into the park today I was looking for serenity.

TERRY. And look what we've given you.

BETTY. And look what he's giving us.

MAY. Lionel, if we had gone ahead with the ceremony and then I found out that our home was the home, well —I'd have to find a way to live with it. We'd have worked it out, but I can't willingly walk into this marriage knowing what I now know.

LIONEL. I see.

MAY. Do you understand?

LIONEL. Yes.

BETTY. Good, let's head to the reservoir. There's got to be a husband there for you.

GINA. We've still got an hour until the reception.

TERRY. We'll have to move fast, then. Let's go!

BETTY. This terrorism is tough on a gal's feet. And the pressure!

COLIN. Listen, Lionel. Sorry things didn't work out.

LIONEL. Me too. It would've been neat to get married today.

TERRY. Lionel, nice to meet you. Take care of yourself.

LIONEL. Thanks, Terry.

GINA. Lionel, listen. About what happened in the kitchen when I was putting together that tray of Bourbon Balls?

LIONEL. Yes?

GINA. Forget it. I won't tell May.

LIONEL. Thanks. Betty?

BETTY. What?

LIONEL. No goodbye?

BETTY. Goodbye.

(*BETTY, GINA, COLIN and TERRY all leave.*)

MAY. Well.

LIONEL. Well.

MAY. This is it, then?

LIONEL. I guess so. But it's your decision.

MAY. I know. And it's a political one.

LIONEL. I wish you'd reconsider.

MAY. I can't.

LIONEL. Sure you can.

MAY. No, I'm afraid it would be too late.

LIONEL. I see.

MAY. I mean, you're crazy.

LIONEL. I am.

MAY. So ...

LIONEL. So.

MAY. What?

LIONEL. What, "What?"?

MAY. You were going to say something?

LIONEL. I was just thinking that there is some lucky unsuspecting single jogger out there who's going to get a special woman as his wife.

MAY. Thanks. See ya.

LIONEL. Uh ... May?

MAY. Yes?

LIONEL Can I give the bride-to-be a good luck kiss?

MAY. Sure. (*THEY kiss.*)

LIONEL. Good luck.

MAY. Same to you. (*MAY leaves.*)

LIONEL. (*Sits down and goes back to his book. After a moment HE looks up.*) Whew! (*HE smiles.*)

(*LIGHTS fade.*)

THE END

COSTUME PLOT

Lionel Stark
Costume: Casual clothes, khaki pants, button down shirt, comfortable shoes—perfect for a Sunday afternoon in Central Park.
Props: A hardback book, maybe Somerset Maugham or Philip Roth.

May Wilder
Costume: A truly beautiful wedding dress, as extravagant as the budget allows—but always tasteful.
Props: A bridal bouquet, three pieces of coordinated luggage, the luggage should be as tasteful as the gown. A small handgun.

Betty Wilder
Costume: A cheerful "dressy" dress, it might have been garish had Betty had her way but May picked it out for her so it's basically tasteful.
Props: A matching purse.

Gina Willis
Costume: She's the bridesmaid, but she wouldn't mind stealing focus, so her dress, while picked out by May, has more sex appeal than what you would expect from a bridesmaid.
Props: A matching purse.

<u>Colin Willis</u>
Costume: A rented tuxedo. Not powder blue—
but it would've been if May or Gina had let him.
Instead it's gray.

Props: A portable cassette player (and a cassette
of Mendelssohn's Wedding March)

<u>Judge Terry Winship</u>
Costume: A stylish dark suit with a great
Armani/retro necktie.

Props: A bible and notes for the ceremony.

www.ingramcontent.com/pod-product-compliance
Lightning Source LLC
Chambersburg PA
CBHW070403120726
47909CB00008B/2979